# THE
# HOAX ON YOU

*Marilyn Singer*

*illustrations by Richard Williams*

HARPER & ROW, PUBLISHERS

## Acknowledgments
### Thanks to Steve Aronson, Jay Kerig, Oak Kerig, Leslie Kimmelman, Andrew Ottiger, and Karl Ottiger.

The Hoax on You

Text copyright © 1989 by Marilyn Singer
Illustrations copyright © 1989 by Richard Williams

1  2  3  4  5  6  7  8  9  10

First Edition

Library of Congress Cataloging-in-Publication Data

Singer, Marilyn.
    The hoax on you / by Marilyn Singer ; illustrated
by Richard Williams.
        p.    cm.—(A Sam and Dave mystery story)
    Summary: When Sam and Dave Bean, amateur detectives, try to find
the person who's been stealing jewelry around the neighborhood,
their suspicions center on a foreign exchange student in their class
at school.
    ISBN 0-06-025850-0 : $      . ISBN 0-06-025851-9 (lib. bdg.) : $
    [1. Mystery and detective stories.   2. Twins—Fiction.]
    I. Williams, Richard, 1950–   ill.  II. Title.  III. Series.
PZ7.S6172Hm  1989                                         88-22004
[Fic]—dc19                                                    CIP
                                                               AC

# THE
# Hoax on You

# 1

"Hey, Sam," said Dave, glancing up from the magazine he was reading. "Do you believe there's life on the moon?"

"Huh?" Sam, his twin brother, looked up, holding his hands stiffly in front of him. His fingers were coated with bits of paper and glue. He was trying to make a birthday card for his friend Rita O'Toole and not doing a very good job of it. Dave had finished his card half an hour ago; it was perfect. "What did you say?" Sam asked.

"I said, do you believe there's life on the moon?"

"No. Nobody does."

"They did in 1835. It says here in *Funtime* magazine that in 1835 a newspaper called *The Sun* printed a bunch of articles which claimed that a British astronomer looked through a new and powerful telescope and saw buffaloes, goats, birds, and, last but not least, furry little winged men on the moon," Dave told him.

"That's ridiculous."

"Yeah. But people believed it—and the newspaper sold lots and lots of copies. That was one successful hoax."

Sam shook his head. "Wow! I wonder how many hoaxes there have been."

"Lots." Dave glanced down at *Funtime.* "Here's one about a guy who fooled everyone into thinking he was a wealthy lord and another about a photographer who claimed he could take pictures of ghosts and other hoaxes too. And pretty soon, because of this magazine, there are going to be a lot more."

"What do you mean?"

"The editors are having a hoax contest. Whoever pulls off the best hoax wins."

"Wow!" Sam exclaimed, clasping his knees. "Do you want to enter it?"

"I don't know. Maybe. It seems to me a pair of identical twins who also happen to be detectives should be able to come up with a pretty good hoax," Dave said, eyes twinkling.

"Yeah!" Sam grinned. He picked up his hand to slap five.

"Yuck!" Dave exclaimed.

Sam looked down at his hand. It was still covered with some paper and glue, but not as much as his knees were. "Oh no. What a mess."

"Better wash your pants before Mom sees them."

Sam nodded, but before he could even get up, he and Dave heard their mother open the front door. Sam swallowed. "You don't suppose," he said slowly, "we could pull a hoax on Mom, switch pants and pretend I'm you, do you?"

"Sam, I don't think Mom would ever believe you're me," Dave said, trying not to grin.

"I was afraid you'd say that." Sam sighed.

# 2

"How about this for our hoax—you pretend you're me and run the next Student Council meeting," Dave suggested as he and Sam walked down the hall to their classrooms.

"No!" Sam yelped. He was shy and would sooner roll in a patch of poison ivy than run a meeting. "You know I couldn't do that," he added in a lower voice.

"Sure you could. Anybody can run a meeting."

Sam shook his head. "No, anybody can't."

"Well then, what do you think we should do?"

Sam thought a minute, then offered, "How about if you pretend you're me and pitch the game against the Sliders next Saturday."

"Forget it!" Dave's voice rose. He would rather eat the school cafeteria's food than pitch a baseball game.

"Why? Anybody can throw a baseball," Sam said, deadpan.

"Okay, okay. I got the message. If we're going to switch, we'll just have to find something we both can do. But we'll have to find it fast. The contest deadline's only three weeks away."

Sam nodded. Then he and Dave reached their room. "We'll work on it later," said Dave, keeping his voice quiet so none of their classmates would overhear their plans.

Ms. Corfein, their teacher, wasn't there yet, but most of the kids were. Sam and Dave took their seats and listened to the chatter around them. It was pretty much the same kind of chatter they heard every day, about who was getting a new bike and which TV actor was cutest and what was the answer to problem three, five, seven, eight, or ten of the math homework. Robbie Tucker was telling Mickey Gillette about a robbery. Someone had stolen his grandma's sapphire earrings. Sam and Dave pricked up their ears at that until they learned that Robbie's grandma lived in another town, so there was no case for Bean Brothers, Private Eyes, to get involved in.

Then suddenly, Trudy Felner bustled into the room. "She's coming!" she shouted, making everyone jump. "She's coming!"

"Who?" asked Tina Larrabee. "Who's coming?"

"Oh, it's so exciting. She's coming today!"

"Who?"

"Dardanella!" Trudy announced.

"Dardanella!" exclaimed Tina.

"Dardanella," other kids buzzed.

"Wow, Dardanella!" yelled Mickey. "Who's she?"

Trudy glared at him. "The foreign exchange student," she said, emphasizing each word.

"Oh, yeah," Mickey said with a straight face. "The one from Cabbage."

"Gabisch!" Trudy, exasperated, hollered.

"Oh, yeah."

Kids giggled. Mickey was a clown. He loved to tease people—and he especially loved to tease Trudy. Dave said it was because he had a crush on her. Sam thought that was a funny way to show it. The few times he'd had a crush on a girl, he'd blushed and gotten all tongue-tied. Dave never blushed or got tongue-tied. But then again, he never got crushes either.

Trudy sniffed and turned to Sam and Dave, who were at that moment giving each other puzzled looks. "Don't you think it's exciting? Dardanella'll be here any minute."

"Yes, I think it's exciting," answered Dave. He and Sam had been looking forward to meeting Dardanella for weeks. They even planned to invite her and their classmate Weezie, whose family she was staying with, to their house for dinner. "But I thought Weezie said Dardanella wouldn't be arriving for two weeks," Dave finished.

"Yesterday morning while Weezie was at school, his dad got a telegram saying Dardanella would be at their house that evening. Weezie called to tell me."

"Weezie called you?" Mickey said, sounding annoyed. "Since when are you friends?"

Dave wondered the same thing. Trudy and Weezie were unlikely buddies. Trudy was a big gossip and she didn't have much of a sense of humor. Weezie McDowell, who'd gotten his nickname because of his odd laugh, never gossiped and was a big practical joker. He loved things like plastic vomit and cameras that squirted water in your face. He bought some of them from a local shop and ordered other things from magazines. Dave hoped he wasn't planning to try any of his jokes on the foreign exchange student. He hoped even more that she wasn't a practical joker too. One in the class was quite enough.

Trudy ignored Mickey and was about to say something else when the classroom door opened.

"There she is!" Tina yelled.

"That's not her," said Robbie Tucker, as Rita O'Toole walked into the room.

Rita looked confused until Dave filled her in on what was happening.

Rita'd been looking forward to meeting Dardanella, too. "I wonder what she's like?" she asked.

"Tall and pretty," said Mickey before Trudy could answer.

"How do you know that? You haven't even seen her," Trudy gibed. "Weezie hadn't even seen her yet when he called me."

"I saw that travel booklet Ms. Corfein passed around. The one with pictures of Cabbage . . ."

"Gabisch!"

"Yeah—and all the girls in the pictures were tall and pretty." He wiggled his eyebrows.

This time everyone laughed, including Sam and Dave.

Then once again the door opened. All the kids excitedly turned to look, and this time they were rewarded. There stood Weezie with a bald wig and a pair of handcuffs on. Next to him was one of the tallest, prettiest girls anyone had ever seen. She had long dark hair, tanned skin, and big blue eyes.

"Hi, everybody," said Weezie. "This is Dardanella."

Dardanella surveyed the room with a dimpled smile. "Hello, every person. I am Dardanella and I am overthrilled to make your acquaintances." Then her eyes lit on Sam and Dave. "I am most happy to meet the famous Beans. Weezie told me much of you. I look forward to learning from your own mouths all about the most interesting cases you have solved." She smiled again.

Sam turned bright red, smiled back briefly, and lowered his eyes. He was waiting for Dave to take over, knowing Dave would know just what to say.

But Dave said nothing. Surprised, Sam turned to look at him and his mouth fell open. Dave was sitting there, fiddling with the bottom of his sweater and grinning the biggest, silliest grin Sam had ever seen.

Sam closed his mouth and clapped his hand over it to stifle the giggle that was about to come out.

Dave, his cool, poised brother Dave, who'd never had a crush in his life, had one now, and it looked like it was going to be a whopper.

# 3

Dave was racing home as fast as he could. He desperately needed to talk to his mother. She was usually pretty understanding. He hoped she'd be understanding now about the two dinner guests who were going to show up at their house in just three hours.

It wasn't like Dave to spring guests on his mom and dad at the last minute. But today he couldn't help it. When Ms. Corfein had arrived in class, she'd urged the class to make Dardanella feel at home. She needn't have bothered. The kids were outdoing each other in welcoming the foreign exchange student, inviting her to enough parties, dinners, dances, outings to last until she had to return to Gabisch. Dave wanted to be the first to welcome her, so he'd quickly invited her to dinner at his house that very evening. Sam had given him a look that said, "What are you doing?" Dave had ignored him, and to his delight, Dardanella and Weezie had accepted the invitation. At least he was delighted until he realized he had to talk to his mom. At lunchtime he tried to reach her by phone. But all he got was a busy signal. He tried again just before gym and got the same thing. So now he had to tell her face to face. And alone. Sam was at baseball practice.

By the time Dave reached his front door, he had a stitch in his side and his lungs felt ready to burst. He took a few slow, deep breaths and went into the house. "Mom! Mom!" he called.

He walked into the kitchen. A man in a uniform with a tool belt around his waist was talking on the telephone. "Yeah, I've got it. It was easy," said the man, not even noticing Dave.

Dave went upstairs. The bathroom door was open and there was a lot of clanking and banging coming from the room. "Mom?" Dave asked, peeking in. A woman in a different kind of uniform was fiddling with the faucets in the shower. She glanced at Dave. "I'm not your mom, kid," she grunted, and went back to work.

Dave frowned and moved on to his parents' room. A man in a suit was sprinkling powder all over the rug. Standing next to him was Dave's mother. Her hair was limp. Her blouse was smudged. Her mouth was frowning. "Look, I agree. It is a fine machine," she said. "But I really don't need . . ."

"Now, this is a wool rug," the man interrupted. "You saw how it cleaned the synthetic carpet downstairs. Now just watch how this baby does wool."

Ms. Bean tried again. "I'm sure it does wool fine, but I don't need another . . ." Her words were drowned out by the roar of the vacuum cleaner. Ms. Bean put her hands to her ears, looked up, and saw Dave.

"Hi, Mom," he shouted, hoping she'd smile. Instead she frowned even more.

"Oh, no. Don't tell me it's already after three o'clock?" she yelled, lowering her hands. "I haven't even gone shopping. We don't have a thing for dinner."

Dave gulped. "Uh . . . dinner . . . I need to talk to you about that."

"What?"

"Dinner!"

"See how it picks up this stuff," the salesman bellowed.

"Well, we'll just have to have leftovers," Ms. Bean shouted.

"No!" hollered Dave.

"What?"

"I mean, I could go shopping."

"Could you? That would be great. Here's my list and some money." She fumbled in her pocket.

"Powder, dirt, grass, leaves, dog hair, paper, you name it, it swallows it . . ."

"But Mom, I have to tell you . . ."

"Not now, Dave. We'll talk when you return."

Well, I'll just have to tell her when I get back, Dave thought. Then he turned and sprinted down the stairs, out the door, and toward the shops, where he planned to set a record as world's fastest grocery buyer.

13

Sam was whistling as he ambled home. Practice had gone really well. Sam's fastball had been working and the curve was coming along. Now he was looking forward to a shower and an interesting dinner with Weezie, Dardanella, and Dave. He still couldn't quite believe that Dave had invited guests to dinner without first getting permission. But knowing him, Sam thought, he's probably smoothed it all over with Mom by now.

He turned up the path to his house. A large, lavender-suited woman carrying a briefcase was walking briskly down it. She and Sam did a little dance, each trying to get out of the other's way.

"Should we try the waltz?" the woman said, smiling.

Sam smiled back, moving to one side and letting her pass. Nice lady, he thought. Then, whistling again, he trotted up the steps, opened the front door, and went inside. "Mom! I'm home," he called.

A big sigh came from the direction of the living room.

Sam headed there and found his mother stretched out on the sofa with her eyes closed. On the coffee table in front of her were three lipsticks, two bottles of nail polish, two containers of eye shadow, three boxes of soap, four bottles of cologne, and a small jug of after-shave lotion. "Thank goodness, that's the last of them," she said.

"The last of what, Mom?" asked Sam.

Ms. Bean opened her eyes. "The phone repair-

man, the plumber, the vacuum cleaner salesman, the Betty Bee lady, and the guy collecting money for retired racehorses, would you believe? I really had trouble getting rid of him. I had to tell him I had company—who was actually the Betty Bee lady I'd left in our bedroom matching lipstick colors to my dresses."

"Looks like you didn't mind the Betty Bee lady that much," Sam said, surveying the array of items on the table.

"Well, most of these are Christmas presents."

"Christmas is eight months away, Mom."

"I'm avoiding the holiday rush," she answered, deadpan.

Sam giggled.

His mother sighed again. "Anyway, she's gone. They're all gone. And now I'm looking forward to a short nap and the four of us having a nice quiet dinner."

A warning bell dinged in Sam's head. "The four of us?" he said.

"That's right."

"Uh . . . Mom, where's Dave?"

"Buying groceries."

"Didn't he . . . uh . . . talk to you when he got home?"

"Talk to me? About what?" She sat up, a suspicious look creeping over her face.

Sam stifled a groan. How come even when I'm not in trouble, I'm in trouble, he wondered. He toyed with the idea of waiting for Dave to return and take the licks for this one. But he knew he couldn't. Dave was his friend as well as his brother. "About the . . . the dinner guests we're having."

"The what?" Her voice rose.

"The dinner guests—Weezie and Dardanella, the new foreign exchange student. She just arrived today."

"Are you kidding?"

Sam shook his head.

"You invited them without asking me first?"

Sam didn't tell her it was Dave's idea. It wouldn't have helped.

"Oh, Sam. What next?" His mother groaned.

Sam said he didn't know. He also didn't know how surprised he was going to be when he found out.

# 4

"I love America so much," Dardanella said as Ms. Bean dished her out a second helping of meat loaf. "The people here are so friendly and considerable."

"*Considerate,*" said Weezie.

"Yes. My English is not very well."

"*Good,*" Weezie corrected.

"Your English is fine," said Ms. Bean, smiling.

Sam smiled too. His mother was no longer in a

bad mood. He tried to catch Dave's eye to exchange a relieved glance, but Dave was too busy looking at Dardanella and grinning his goofy grin.

Right now he wouldn't notice if a tornado picked us all up and took us to Oz, Sam thought. But he didn't mind. Dave had honorably told their mother it was his idea and not Sam's to invite Weezie and Dardanella for dinner. Then he'd made most of the meal. By the time Weezie and Dardanella arrived, Ms. Bean didn't look so miserable. Weezie's false hand, which dropped off when she shook it, wasn't a big hit with her, but Dardanella's gift of a small box of chocolates was. And so was Dardanella.

"And everything is so big here," Dardanella went on now. "Your automobile . . ." she said to Sam and Dave's father, an easygoing man with a good sense of humor. "You may sleep in it."

"Only when my wife and I have a fight," he said.

Dardanella looked puzzled.

"That was a joke," Weezie told her.

"Oh. Oh, I have it."

"You mean you *get* it."

"Get what?"

"Never mind," said Weezie.

After a pause, Dardanella turned to Ms. Bean. "Your house it is large too. And full of pretty things."

Sam and Dave had given Dardanella and Weezie a grand tour of the house. Dardanella had oohed and aahed over everything—the old vase in the living room, the carpet on the stairs, the aquarium, Dave's model planes, Sam's baseball glove, their father's collection of hats, their mother's jewelry case.

"And so clean . . . My mother scrubs all day, but our house, it can't be so clean with the goats and chickens in and out, in and out." Dardanella laughed. So did everyone else.

Everyone except Sam. "Goats and chickens?" he said. "You keep goats and chickens in the city?"

Dardanella blinked at him. "The city?"

"Weezie told us in class that you live in the city."

She glanced briefly at Weezie. To Sam's surprise, she seemed annoyed. But then she turned back to Sam. "Ah, yes. But our city is like your country." She smiled and daintily began to finish her dinner.

After everyone was through eating, Sam and Dave took Weezie and Dardanella back up to their room. Sam began to show Weezie his baseball card collection. Dave opened his closet and lifted out a wooden box. "We can set this up in the den," he said to Dardanella.

"What is it?" she asked.

"My chess set."

"Chess?" Dardanella wrinkled her nose.

Sam stopped what he was doing and stared at her.

Dave didn't seem to notice. "I know you're president of your chess club and I'm not a very good player, but I thought you'd like to play anyway. Maybe you could teach me a gambit or two."

Sam saw Dardanella glance again at Weezie, and this time she was clearly bugged.

Weezie didn't look back at her. "Why don't we *all* play something?" he said quickly. "Something American—like Monopoly."

"Monopoly?" Dave's brow puckered. He didn't much like Monopoly. He thought it was silly and boring.

But Dardanella said, "Oh, yes. Monopoly. I want to learn that game."

Stifling a sigh, Dave put away the chess set and took down the Monopoly game, which they all played for the next hour and a half until Dardanella wiped everyone off the board.

"She's interesting, isn't she?" said Dave later that night as he and his brother got ready for bed. "So smart and . . . pretty."

Sam didn't say anything. Something about Dardanella was bothering him. She was interesting all right. And smart and pretty. But . . . "Dave, don't you think she acted a little funny?" he asked slowly.

"Funny?" Dave gave him a puzzled look.

"Yes. When I told her I thought she lived in the city and when you asked her to play chess and the way she played Monopoly—beating us all like that when she said she'd never played the game before."

"So? She's a fast learner, and as for the other things, I think Weezie got some information wrong . . ."

"But he got that information from her letters."

"So? He could've misunderstood them."

Sam gave up and got into bed.

20

Dave did too, and in a few minutes he was sound asleep.

But Sam lay there thinking for a long time. Then he got thirsty and went to get a drink of water. As he passed his parents' room, he heard his mother's voice behind the door.

"I'm telling you, Ben. I've looked everywhere for my emerald ring and I can't find it."

"Ellen," his father replied, "did you check your jewelry case thoroughly?"

"Yes, and it's not there. It's not in any of my drawers either."

"Well, I know you won't get any sleep until it turns up—which means neither will I. So let's both look for it, okay?"

Sam rolled his eyes and moved on to the bathroom. His mother was always misplacing some piece of jewelry or another. Once Dave found one of her silver earrings in their fish tank. "I guess it fell off when I was trying to count the baby guppies," she'd told him. Another time Sam discovered her gold necklace in their big dictionary. "I was using it for a bookmark," she'd said sheepishly. Sam hoped the ring turned up fast this time. He drank his water and returned to his room.

"Is it time to get up yet?" Dave asked groggily.

"No. Go back to sleep," Sam told him. He wished he could sleep too, but he was still wondering about Dardanella. Think about something else, he ordered himself. Think about the hoax contest. You and Dave still haven't come up with any good ideas for it.

So Sam thought about the contest—and it worked like a charm. He didn't come up with any good ideas, but in less than five minutes he was as fast asleep as Dave.

# 5

Several days had passed. Dardanella's popularity was still growing, and so was Dave's crush. He tried to keep it a secret from the other guys in his class, but they were beginning to notice—and to tease him about it.

"Hey, look at Bean. He's all dressed up!" Mickey Gillette would say in class. "You think maybe he's trying to impress someone?"

"Sure looks like it," Robbie Tucker would play along. "Wonder who it could be?"

Then they'd both crane their heads at Dardanella and laugh.

Or they'd catch Dave in the boys' room and Mickey would say, "Hey, Tucker. Bean's combing his hair again. How many times does that make it today?"

"Five at least, Gillette," Robbie'd answer.

"Yeah, well it's a good thing though, because just

this morning Dardanella told me that Dave Bean has the weirdest hair she's ever seen. So maybe if he combs it another five times he'll finally get it to look right."

Dave tried to laugh along with them, but it was hard.

Even harder to deal with was the way Sam was behaving around Dardanella. Sam had said he thought Dardanella was acting funny. To Dave it was Sam who was acting funny, like he was studying her or something. It was starting to bother Dave. And that bothered him even more. Sam was not only his brother, but his best friend—and the last thing Dave wanted was to be angry at his best friend.

Sam, for his part, was upset too. He was used to talking about everything with Dave. But now he couldn't. Dave didn't want to hear Sam's suspicions about Dardanella—suspicions that were growing daily.

Yesterday Dardanella had talked about her brother, Ladislo, who wanted to join the Gabischian army. "I thought Gabisch didn't have an army," said Rita O'Toole.

"It is a very little army," said Dardanella swiftly.

"But the encyclopedia says it doesn't have one at all," Rita persisted.

"How old is this encyclopedia?" asked Dardanella.

"Three years old."

"Ah, well, the army it is very new," said Dardanella.

Rita let the matter go, but Sam was not so easily convinced.

And then this morning Ms. Corfein brought in her guitar and asked Dardanella to play a Gabischian folk song. "You must be a fine guitarist. Weezie said you've been playing for four years."

"Oh, no. I am not fine. Not fine at all," Dardanella protested.

However, Ms. Corfein pressed her until she finally gave in. "But because we are in America I will play an American song," she said. She took the guitar and banged out what Sam thought was the worst rendition of "You Are My Sunshine" he'd ever heard until he realized it was actually the worst rendition of "She'll Be Comin' 'Round the Mountain" he'd ever heard. Then Dardanella made a joke about it, and everyone laughed. But Sam felt uncomfortable and wary inside.

Now it was lunchtime. Sam, Dave, and Rita were sharing a table with Weezie, Dardanella, Tina, Trudy, and Mickey. Dave, as usual, was paying attention only to Dardanella. Sam was paying attention to everybody.

He saw Weezie put fake bugs into Mickey's food, laughed at a silly joke Mickey told, watched Dardanella smile enthusiastically at something Dave said to her, checked out Rita's latest cipher book, heard Trudy compliment Tina on her nail polish.

"It's called 'Precious Pink,' " Tina told her. "Mom got it for me from the Betty Bee lady. She matched the polish to my clothes and some to Mom's clothes

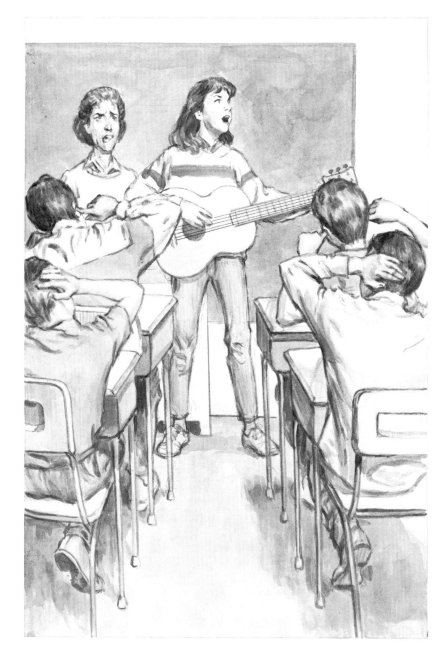

too. Mom said she learned a lot about color and would have learned even more if they hadn't been interrupted by some nut collecting money for retired racehorses. Anyway, right after I put the polish on, my little sister spilled half the bottle all over the rug. Dad was furious—even the superdooper vacuum cleaner he'd bought the same day from this other door-to-door salesman doesn't clean up nail polish. Then, on top of everything, this expensive watch of his disappeared."

Sam's skin suddenly began to prickle. With his sandwich halfway to his mouth, he stared so hard at Tina that she turned her head and looked at him.

"What is it, Sam? Do I have mayonnaise on my chin or something?"

"No, it's . . . Did you say your dad's missing his watch?"

"Yes. Why? Are you and Dave going to do some detection and find it or something?"

Sam glanced at Dave. He was still deep in conversation with Dardanella. "Or something," Sam said.

Tina waited for him to go on, but when he didn't, she shrugged and turned back to Trudy.

Mr. Larrabee's watch gone. And Mom's ring—it still hadn't shown up. Absentmindedly, Sam took a bite of his sandwich. Of course it still might. And, anyway, what possible connection could there be between the two things, he thought. But his skin was still tingling.

And then Tina said, "Boy, Dad was really in a bad mood. He kept asking me if I or my guests had seen the watch. I hadn't. And I told him Weezie and Dardanella hadn't either."

Sam's head shot up. The sandwich fell out of his hand. He turned his head and stared at Dardanella, but he wasn't seeing her there, now, in the cafeteria. He was seeing her three days ago in his parents' room, running her hand back and forth over the top of his mother's velvet-covered jewelry box.

# 6

"That's crazy. Totally crazy." Dave, hands on hips, glared at Sam.

"It's not," Sam said softly. "She could have taken Mom's ring while we were both showing Weezie Dad's hats. She could have taken Tina's father's watch while she was visiting there."

"I don't want to hear any more of this," Dave said. "First you tell me Dardanella's been acting funny. Then you give me some evidence that isn't evidence at all. Now you expect me to believe that she's a thief. What I think is you don't like her. And the reason you don't is because she likes me better than you."

Sam stared in shock. He knew lots of brothers who were jealous of each other. But aside from a little twinge here and there, he'd never been really jealous of Dave. And Dave knew that. At least the old Dave did.

For another moment neither of them said a thing. Then, brushing a bit of lint off his sweater, Dave said, "Are you still going to Trudy's party?"

Not trusting his voice, Sam nodded.

"Well, we'd better leave, then, or we'll be late." Dave turned and walked out of the room.

Sam stood up and began to follow him. On his way to the door he glanced at his desk. There was a framed photo there of the Bean Brothers and their Aunt Margaret in Papagayo, Texas. Aunt Margaret was laughing. Sam and Dave were wearing Stetson hats and grinning at each other. Sam's eyes began to water. He turned quickly away from the photo and, shoulders hunched, trudged out of the room.

"Good party, isn't it?" Tina asked Sam, who was sitting in a corner.

He nodded. It seemed to him that's all he'd been doing for the past few hours—sitting in a corner and nodding.

He and Dave had gotten there early too—just as a familiar-looking vacuum cleaner salesman was leaving. Trudy was still polishing her nails, so they didn't have anyone to talk to but each other, which they didn't feel like doing. But even when the other kids showed up, Sam hardly talked to anybody. He had, however, kept an eye on Dardanella. So far she hadn't left the room.

"This punch is really good," said Tina.

"Yeah." Sam took a sip from the cup he'd hardly touched.

"You find out anything about my dad's watch yet?"

Sam paused a second, then said, "No. Not yet."

"Well, let me know if you do. He's still in a bad mood about it."

"Okay."

Tina drifted away and Rita O'Toole came over. Sam got ready to nod again. But Rita said, "What's wrong with you? You look like you just lost your best friend."

Sam made a funny sound that was somewhere between a laugh and a sob, and without even knowing it, his eyes flickered in Dave's direction.

Rita noticed. "Did you and Dave have a fight?" she asked.

"No . . . yes . . . well, sort of," Sam stammered.

"What was it about?"

Sam hesitated. On the one hand, he didn't want to talk about it. On the other, Rita was a good friend, and right now he needed one. "Well," he began, clearing his throat.

But before he could say anything he saw Dardanella leaving the room.

"Excuse me," he told Rita, leaping to his feet.

Pushing through the crowd, he opened the door and stepped out into the hall. It was deserted. Where'd she go? he wondered. He moved slowly down the hall. All the doors were closed and he couldn't hear anything behind them. Then he came to one door that was slightly ajar, and as he leaned toward it, he heard a familiar voice say, "Sam, what are you doing?"

He turned. Dave was standing there, frowning at him. "N—nothing," he stuttered.

"I don't believe you," Dave said.

Suddenly the door opened and they heard a scream.

Both boys jumped and whirled around to see Dardanella clutching her throat. "Oh my, you frightened me. I was looking to wash my hands. They are all sticky from punch. But this is not where to do it," she said.

Sam and Dave glanced over her shoulder and saw Trudy's parents' bedroom behind her.

"It's next door," Dave said, pointing to the room he'd just come from.

"Thank you, my most helpful friend." Dardanella beamed and went into the bathroom.

Feeling Dave's eyes on him, Sam walked stiffly back into the den. His seat in the corner was unoccupied. He sank into it and a loud, embarrassing noise whooshed out. Weezie, leaning against the wall near him, began to laugh along with several other kids. Sam stood up. On the chair was a small pillow. "Whoopee Cushion," it read. "Guaranteed to pep up any party." Sam handed it over to Weezie.

"Good joke, huh?" Weezie said, still laughing.

Sam thought about telling Weezie what he really thought of the joke, but instead he just sat back down and nodded.

The party went on and on. Kids talked and played video games. Someone put on music. Weezie played practical jokes. Rita had to leave early because she had to stay with her brother, Leroy. Sam, still in his corner, never got to tell her what was bothering him. Dardanella danced with a lot of boys, but with Dave the most. And Dave felt really proud. This is the best party I've even been to, he thought—or would be if it weren't for Sam. He cast a guilty look his brother's way. He couldn't believe Sam was so jealous. That wasn't like him at all. But what other explanation could there be for the awful things he'd said?

"Okay, everybody." Trudy clapped her hands. "Now it's time for a surprise to welcome our guest from Gabisch." She opened the door wide.

"Oh good, it's time for the cake," Mickey said loudly, and some kids laughed.

"We're ready, Mom," Trudy called.

There was a brief pause, and then Ms. Felner came into the room. In her hand she held, instead of a cake, a cardboard box. "All right, who took it?" she said in a loud, trembling voice.

"Mom!" Trudy gasped. "Mom, what are you talking about?"

"I'm talking about this." Ms. Felner took the top off the box and held it upside down. Nothing fell out.

"An empty shoe box?" whispered Mickey.

Ms. Felner heard him. "That's right. It's empty now. But it wasn't empty this morning. This morning it had my pearl necklace and earrings inside. I know because I checked, like I do every day. Someone went into my bedroom, found the box, and took my necklace and earrings. Which one of you was it?" She stood there furiously, waiting.

But no one said a word. In the silence, Sam tried to see how Dardanella was reacting. But her back was to him. Then he felt someone looking at him. He turned his head and met Dave's eyes. They wore the saddest expression Sam had ever seen.

# 7

"Maybe it was someone else," Sam said.

Slumped on a park bench, Dave stared at the ground and said nothing.

The two had left Trudy's party a little while ago. When no one came forward with the jewelry, Trudy's mother said she'd give the culprit until tomorrow evening to return the necklace and earrings, no questions asked. If her jewelry was not returned by then, she'd call the police. Then she had told everyone to leave. Not wanting to go straight home, Sam and Dave had gone to the park.

"Maybe somebody else was in all three places—our house, Tina's, and Trudy's—and took the stuff," Sam continued. Funny, he thought. Now that it seems even more likely that Dardanella did it, here I am trying to find reasons why she didn't. "We don't have any proof," he added weakly.

"She had opportunity and motive—her family's poor," Dave responded dully.

Sam refrained from saying he wasn't sure how much of what Dardanella had told them about her family—or anything else—was true. Instead, softly, he asked, "Dave, what do you think we should do?"

Dave was silent for a long time. Then at last, he answered in the same flat voice, "Talk to Weezie. And lay a trap."

"How are we going to get Weezie alone? He's almost always with Dardanella."

"It won't be hard. Dardanella told me Tina was taking her to buy her first pair of American sneakers tonight right after the party. Weezie isn't joining them. If we go over there now we can catch him alone," Dave explained. But he didn't budge.

"Well then, I guess we'd better go," Sam urged him gently.

Dave stayed put. Still staring down, he said, "Sam, I . . . I'm sorry for the way I've been acting with you. I feel bad about it."

"It's okay," Sam told him, patting his shoulder. "It's okay, Dave."

They stayed that way for another minute. Then, straightening up, Dave said, "Okay. Let's go."

Together, Bean Brothers, Private Eyes, rose and headed toward Weezie's house.

"He'll be down in a minute," said Weezie's dad, leading Sam and Dave into the living room, "as soon as he gets the disappearing ink that didn't disappear out of his bedspread. Just make yourselves comfortable in the meantime."

"Thank you," said Dave.

He and Sam sat down on the sofa. In front of them on the coffee table was a photo album. It was open to a page of recent photos of Weezie and Dardanella. One picture showed Dardanella demonstrating a Gabischian dance step she'd shown Dave just today. Dave winced; without thinking, he quickly turned the page. When he realized Weezie's dad was looking at him, he covered up by saying, "Good photographs. Who took them?"

"I did," Mr. McDowell answered rather proudly. "It's my hobby. I like to take portraits. Dardanella is a good model. In fact, she asked me to take lots of photos of her to send home."

Knowing how Dave was feeling, Sam pointed to a picture of a little dark-haired girl on the adjacent page. Golden sunlight on her face, the girl was picking bright oranges from a tree. More fruit lay scattered on the ground all around her feet. "I like this photo," Sam said.

"That's Weezie's cousin, Cynthia. A lively kid. She lives in Florida. We haven't seen her since she was five, but she's finally coming to visit us next week for Easter vacation. Between her and Dardanella, we're going to have a full house."

"Boy, am I going to write that company and tell them . . . Oh, hi, Sam and Dave," Weezie said, as he entered the room. His hands were stained dark blue and there was a blue streak across his forehead. "What are you guys doing here?" He looked at Dave and said pointedly, "Dardanella's gone shopping."

"We wanted to see you," Dave said.

"Well, I'll leave you boys alone. Got to develop some negatives." Weezie's dad left.

"That was some weird party, huh?" Weezie remarked, rubbing at his hands. "Darn, this stuff . . . At least the end of it was. . . . This'll never come off. . . . What did you guys want to talk to me about?"

"The end of the party," Dave said.

"Huh?"

"Dardanella," said Sam. "We . . . uh . . . we think there's . . . we think she's not what she seems."

Weezie's face went all funny then, sort of sheepish. "You don't?" he squeaked. "What do you think she is?"

"We think she . . . uh . . . might be a . . . thief."

Weezie stared first at Sam, then at Dave. Then he began to laugh. "Oh, no. Oh, no. That's ridiculous!"

Sam and Dave didn't laugh with him. "It isn't," Dave said gravely, and he explained why.

But Weezie just kept on laughing. "Dardanella . . . *wheeze wheeze* . . . a thief . . . *wheeeze.*"

"It isn't funny," Dave said sharply.

Suddenly, Weezie stopped giggling. Another odd expression flickered across his face, but this one looked more shrewd than sheepish. "How are you going to prove it? You want to search her room?"

Dave turned to Sam. Sam shook his head. Neither of them felt right about doing that.

"We're going to lay a trap," Sam said. "At Rita O'Toole's house. Tomorrow. Will you bring Dardanella over there at two o'clock?"

"Okay," Weezie agreed.

Sam and Dave got up to leave. "We hope we're wrong, Weezie," Dave said.

"I'm sure you are," Weezie replied, lips twitching. "I'm positively sure you are."

As Sam and Dave walked out the door, they heard him burst into laughter once again.

*Tap tap tap.* Dave drummed his fingers on the coffee table. *Tap tap tap.*

"You're doing it again," Rita said.

Dave looked down at his hand and clenched it. "Sorry," he said.

"We have to try to act natural," Sam said gently.

Dave nodded, but he was thinking, How do you act natural when you're about to try to expose as a crook a girl you really, really liked?

"Now, let me make sure I've got this right," Rita said. "The brooch is on the end table near the sofa. My parents and Leroy won't be back for a while, so we should have no disturbances. When I go into the kitchen to get refreshments, one of you will offer to help and the other one will get Weezie out of sight of the brooch so that Dardanella's left alone with it. Is that right?"

"Right," said Sam.

*Tap tap tap* was Dave's answer. Sam and Rita turned and stared at him. He slapped his hand with the other one. "Right," he said. They all smiled.

But the smiles didn't last long, because the doorbell rang.

"They're here. Are you ready?" asked Rita.

"Yes," said Sam.

"No," whispered Dave. Sam heard him and squeezed his shoulder.

Rita rose, left the room, and returned a few moments later with Dardanella and Weezie, who had his pair of handcuffs dangling from his belt.

"My, it is warm today. It is almost weather to swim in," Dardanella was saying.

"Do you like to swim?" asked Rita.

"Oh, yes. It is one of my favorite things. Especially in the ocean."

"The ocean? But Gabisch isn't near an ocean."

39

"No, that is true. I swim when we go on vacation."
Dardanella looked at Sam and Dave. "Ah, just the
five of us," she said. "How nice." She smiled at Dave
and sat down next to him. The end table with the
brooch was right at her elbow, but she didn't glance
at it. She just kept gazing at Dave and smiling.

He tried to smile back, but his mouth felt stuck.

There was a short but awkward silence. Then
Weezie remarked, "Hey, Rita, I didn't know you
had any pets."

"I don't," she answered.

"Then what's that?" He pointed to a large gray
rat on the rug.

"Yours, I think," Rita told him, picking it up and
handing it to him.

"Can I see it?" asked Sam. He took the rat and
examined it. It was made of rubber, but it looked
quite real. "This is a good fake. Where'd you get
it?"

"Ordered it. From a magazine."

"Which one?"

"*Funtime.*"

"Oh, Dave reads that," Sam said, setting the rat
on the coffee table. "Right, Dave?"

"It must be a good magazine, then," said Dardanella, beaming again.

This time Dave's mouth worked better, but the
grin he gave Dardanella looked more like a jack-o'-
lantern's than his own happy one. I can't stand much
more of this, he thought.

So he was grateful when Rita finally said, "Well, I think I'll get us some refreshments." He jumped up, yelled, "I'll help," and nearly ran out of the room before Rita moved.

Poor Dave, Sam thought. Poor Dave. I hope Dardanella *isn't* the thief. Well, we'll soon find out. I've just got to get Weezie out of the . . . Oh no, how am I going to get Weezie out of the room? I forgot to figure that one out. He wracked his brain.

". . . all right?" Dardanella said.

Sam stared at her. "What? I mean, excuse me? Did you say something?"

"I asked if you're all right. You took a funny breath."

"Oh, yes, I'm fine. I was just worried about my . . . my . . . bike! I think it might have a flat. Hey, Weezie, could you help me with it?"

"Me? I don't know anything about bikes. I don't even own one."

"That doesn't matter." Sam crossed over to Weezie and practically pulled him out of his chair. "You can help me anyway." He steered the shorter boy out of the room.

"What the heck's going on?" Weezie asked as they passed into the kitchen where Rita and Dave were rattling a lot of dishes.

"Shh. It's the trap. We have to leave Dardanella alone in the living room with the brooch. We didn't tell you beforehand because we wanted the trap to look natural."

"That sure looked natural," Weezie said dryly. "If I were a thief, I'd never guess you were trying to catch me in the act."

Sam and Dave shook their heads at each other. Weezie was right. The Bean Brothers were good private eyes, but rotten liars.

"We should give her another few minutes," Rita said, looking at the wall clock.

They all followed her gaze. Boy, it's amazing how slow a few minutes can go, thought Sam.

Finally, Dave exhaled. "Okay. It's time." He strode toward the door.

Rita nodded, picked up the tray of refreshments she'd fixed, and followed him, with Weezie and Sam at her heels.

Dardanella was sitting in exactly the same spot on the sofa she'd been sitting in before. She gave them a big smile. "Ah, orange juice. My favorite. We drink it all the time in Gabisch. Healthy, no? How is your bike?"

No one answered her. They were all staring at the end table where the brooch had been. It wasn't there any longer.

Weezie clapped his hand over his mouth. Rita looked grim. Sam and Dave both sighed.

"It's all over, Dardanella," Sam said. "You might as well come clean."

"Come clean?" Dardanella smiled at him. "Am I dirty?"

"*Come clean* means to confess," rasped Dave. His

throat hurt and his eyes were stinging. "To tell the truth. It's time for you to tell the truth. We know you took the brooch."

"Brooch?"

"The piece of jewelry that was on this table just before. You took it—and Trudy's mother's necklace and earrings, Tina's dad's watch, and our mom's ring, didn't you?"

Dardanella was still smiling. "Brooch. Funny word." She stood up and headed toward the door.

"Where are you going? You can't leave." Sam moved to block her.

Gracefully, she turned toward a small cabinet, pulled open a drawer, and took out something. "Is this what you're looking for?" She held up the brooch.

Sam, Dave, and Rita stared, dumbstruck.

"It seemed not safe to have such pretty jewelry lying around with a thief about."

"You mean . . . you mean you're not a thief?" Dave managed to choke out.

Suddenly, Weezie took his hand from his mouth and, with a great explosion of laughter, collapsed onto the sofa. "Dardanella the thief! Dardanella the thief!" he gasped. "I told you if we could fool Sam and Dave we'd have it made. Well, we did. We fooled them for a whole week—and we're still fooling everyone else. Ha ha ha! We'll win! We'll win for sure!"

"Win? What's he talking about?" asked Rita.

And all at once, Sam knew. "You . . . you're not

from Gabisch. You're not a foreign exchange student. And your name's not Dardanella. You're . . . you're a hoax!"

"What?" said Dave. Then his eyes widened. "A hoax! The contest! The *Funtime* magazine contest. You and Weezie are in this together. Weezie told Trudy first that Dardanella was coming because he knew Trudy would gossip and get everyone all excited. And you made friends with Dave and me because of what Weezie just said—if you could fool us, you could fool anyone."

"You got it!" exclaimed Dardanella. "Or should I say, you *have* it!"

"And we'll win it!" Weezie shouted.

They both laughed.

Sam and Dave didn't know whether to laugh or cry or both, so they just stood there until Dardanella said at last, "Okay, Bean Brothers, Private Eyes, nice work. But that leaves you with two other questions. The first is: If I'm not Dardanella, who am I?"

"I think I can answer that," Sam replied slowly. "You're Weezie's cousin Cynthia from Florida."

"Excellent." She curtsied. "But you can keep calling me Dardanella until the real one shows up. I've gotten used to the name."

Weezie giggled. Then, hiccuping, he asked, "What's the second question?"

Dardanella gestured to Dave.

He cleared his throat. "The second question is: Since Dardanella is innocent, who's the real thief?"

# 9

"How can we find out who the real thief is?" Weezie asked a few moments later.

"We start with deduction," Dave answered.

"Like Sherlock Holmes." Dardanella clapped her hands together. Her eyes shone and she looked prettier than ever.

Dave glanced at her. He felt hurt by Dardanella's pretending to like him just to win a contest—and at the same time he thought she was awfully clever. He pushed away all his feelings. There was no time for them now. There was time only for detection. He turned to Sam and saw that his brother was ready to get right down to business. "Yesterday you said maybe somebody besides Dardanella was in all three places where jewelry was stolen—Trudy's, Tina's, and our house. Let's start with who was at our house the day Mom's ring disappeared."

"There were a bunch of people," Sam responded. "Mom was in a bad mood because of them."

Dave nodded. "Right. There was a telephone repairman. When I got home, he was on the kitchen phone saying something like, 'I've got it. It was easy.'"

"Hmmm. The words sound suspicious, but I don't think he's our thief. The phone was broken, he did fix it, and we could easily check him out with the company—something he'd know," Sam said.

Dave nodded. "I agree. Then there was the plumber. She was working on the shower. We can easily check her out too if we have to, but I don't think she's our thief either. Which brings us to the vacuum cleaner salesman. He was in Mom and Dad's bedroom when I got home."

"He was also at Trudy's the day of the party. Remember? Her mother was trying to get rid of him when we arrived," said Sam.

"He was at Tina's, too. Her dad bought a vacuum from him," said Weezie. "He was showing it off when Dardanella and I got there."

"Wow!" Dardanella exclaimed. "I'll bet it's him."

"It could be," said Dave.

"But," added Rita with her usual sensibleness, "did he have the opportunity to steal the jewelry?"

"What do you mean?" asked Dardanella.

"Was he left alone in the room where the jewelry was? Mr. and Ms. Bean's bedroom, for example?"

"I don't know. But we can find out. Now, have we forgotten any other suspects?"

"Yes. The Betty Bee lady," Sam put in, remembering the pleasant lavender-suited woman. "She was leaving our house when I arrived. She was at Tina's, too, the day her dad's watch disappeared. I heard Tina talking about her. I'm not sure about Trudy's . . ."

"She was at Trudy's the day of the party," Rita said. "I heard Trudy talking to Tina about the new nail polish she'd bought. She didn't want her mother to know about it—her mother thinks makeup's a waste of money."

"Then it could be the Betty Bee lady who's the thief," Weezie stated. "She was in all three places too."

"But did *she* have the opportunity? Was she left alone with the jewelry?" Dardanella nodded at Rita.

There was silence for a moment and then Sam's eyes widened. "The retired-racehorse collector!" he exclaimed.

"Huh?" Everyone stared at him.

Sam opened his mouth to explain, when suddenly the doorbell rang.

"Who could that be?" Rita frowned. "Leroy better not have forgotten his key again." She left the room, went to the door, and peered through the peephole.

In a moment she was back, looking a bit pale under her freckles.

"Who is it?" Dave asked.

"What's wrong?" asked Sam.

Rita swallowed. "It's the Betty Bee lady. What are we going to do now?"

# 10

"Come in, come in," Dardanella's voice rang out grandly. "Mother isn't home right now, but I have my own money and I am very interested in seeing your products."

From behind the living room drapes, Sam and Rita peeked at each other with expressions that said they were afraid Dardanella was overdoing it. They hadn't rehearsed the plan they'd come up with after the bell rang and Sam hurriedly explained his theory about how the robberies were pulled off. They hadn't had time. I hope the plan works, Sam thought, knowing Rita was thinking the same thing. Then Dardanella and the Betty Bee lady entered the room, and Sam and Rita got as stiff and still as the walls they were pressed against.

"Won't you sit down," Dardanella said, motioning to a place on the sofa right next to the end table. Sitting on it in plain sight was the sparkling diamond brooch.

"Thank you," said the Betty Bee lady without once glancing at the table.

What if she never sees it? Sam wondered.

"Nail polish," said Dardanella. "I'm definitely interested in nail polish."

"Well, we have some lovely shades . . ." The Betty Bee lady opened her case and began to take out her samples.

Trying to ignore an itch between his shoulders, Sam prayed he wasn't in for a long wait. He knew that outside in the bushes Dave was praying exactly the same thing.

———

"You really think Sam's right?" Weezie whis-

pered from behind the thick privet hedge near the steps.

"Yes," said Dave from his bush. "It's the only thing that makes sense."

The two boys had slipped out the back door and then raced around to the front when Dardanella let the Betty Bee lady into the house.

"But we've been hiding here for twenty minutes. My legs are beginning to ache and . . ."

"Shhh," said Dave. "I don't think we'll have to wait much longer." Peering between the leaves he saw a short, wiry man nearing the front door. The man had a large collection can in his right hand and a tape recorder in his left. When he got to the door, he tucked the tape recorder under his arm and rang the bell.

In a few moments the door opened. From where he was hiding, Dave couldn't see Dardanella, but he could hear her voice.

"Yes?" she said. "May I help you?"

Dave held his breath.

"Hello. Are your parents home, sweetheart?" the man said in a surprisingly deep voice.

"No. But perhaps I can help you."

"Perhaps you can." He flicked on the tape recorder—and suddenly Dave, Weezie, and Dardanella were right in the middle of a horse race.

The Betty Bee lady still hadn't looked at the end table. Sam was sweating now. It was hot behind the curtain and the itch on his back had gotten worse.

Please. Take the brooch, please, he thought, and was immediately upset with himself. You want her to be a thief? That nice lady? What he really wanted was to give himself a good scratch. He turned his head a tiny bit so he could see Rita out of the corner of his eye. She looked uncomfortable too.

From the front door came the distant noise of something that sounded like horses' hooves and voices yelling. Sam blinked. The guy must have some weird pitch. No wonder Mom thought he was a nut. Then he focused on the Betty Bee lady.

She had opened her purse and taken out a large hanky. She unfolded the hanky carefully, humming to herself. Sam held his breath and watched her. She looked right in his direction and smiled.

Oh no, he thought.

But then, without even turning her head, she whipped her arm out, grabbed the brooch with the handkerchief, and stuffed the whole thing back into her purse faster than a lizard catching a fly.

Sam was so stunned it took him—and Rita—a full fifteen seconds to do what they had to do next— run out from behind the drapes, grab hold of the handbag and the startled thief's arms, and yell "Hoax!" as loud as they could.

"Hoax!" Dardanella shouted.

"I beg your pardon," said the little man. "This is no hoax. Poor Sweet Potato Pie was a winner and where is she now—stuck in a little barn somewhere. Is that a fitting end for a retired racehorse? No . . . whoa!" His breath whooshed out as Dave leaped on

52

his back, knocking him to the ground.

"The handcuffs, Weezie!" Dave commanded as the man began to struggle. "Quick, the handcuffs!"

"They're stuck!" Weezie yelled, fumbling with the pair.

The little man was wrestling with Dave now. He was much stronger than Dave thought he'd be. He was halfway to his feet when Dardanella shrieked, "Oh, no, you don't!" and jumped on him. But he tossed her off like a sweater. Dave was still holding one of the man's legs, but the other was kicking him in the side. "Ow! Weezie! Come on, Weezie!"

"Got 'em!" Weezie bellowed, at last getting hold of the man's arm and clicking one of the cuffs around his left wrist. The man swung at him with his free hand, which Dave managed to grab and force down to Weezie, who neatly fastened the other cuff around it. Then the man gave a tremendous shove and would have gotten away if Dardanella hadn't neatly thrown the rubber rat she'd been hiding in her pocket at his face.

"Ahhh!" he screamed—and tripped.

Dave and Weezie promptly sat on top of him, which was exactly the way the police found them just five minutes after Dardanella called them.

# 11

"My dad says thanks a lot. He got his watch back, you know," Tina told Sam on the last day of school before Easter vacation.

"We know," said Sam. The police had found a whole cache of jewelry in the Betty Bee lady's car . . . Tina's dad's watch, Trudy's mom's necklace and earrings, and Sam and Dave's mother's ring among them.

"Even though she didn't get her earrings back, my grandma thanks you too," said Robbie Tucker. "The Betty Bee lady sure got around. She hit five towns near here. She and her accomplice—the re-tired-racehorse guy. They had a good scam going. He distracted the victim while she grabbed the loot."

Sam nodded a bit grimly. He didn't know about the racehorse collector, but he still couldn't quite believe that that nice woman was a crook. People were awfully disappointing sometimes.

Dave was thinking the exact same thing—but not about the Betty Bee lady. Instead he was gazing at Dardanella's empty seat. She was gone. She'd left for Florida yesterday at about the same time Dave had tossed his copy of *Funtime* magazine into the trash can—and she hadn't even called to say good-bye.

Sighing, he unzipped his backpack and took out

his science book to take his mind off her. But when he opened the book, an envelope fell out. It was addressed to him.

"What's that?" Sam asked.

"I'll let you know in a minute," Dave answered, ripping it open. Inside was a note and photo. The note said:

> *Dear Dave,*
>     *I pretended to be someone I wasn't. But I didn't pretend to like you. I really do.*
>                 *Your friend,*
>                 *Dardanella*
> *P.S. Florida is a nice state. Maybe Bean Brothers, Private Eyes, could take a vacation here sometime soon.*

The photo was of Dardanella. She was smiling, as usual, but it was a friendly, open smile—a smile that didn't lie.

It made Dave smile too—all the way down to his feet.

"I bet I can guess who that's from," Sam said, grinning.

"I'll show it to you later, okay?"

"Okay."

Suddenly there was an excited buzz in the room.

"Hey, Weezie, who's that? It couldn't be Dardanella One—she went home. And I thought you said Dardanella Two wasn't arriving until after vacation," Mickey's voice rang out.

Sam and Dave quickly looked up. There in the

doorway were Weezie, wearing a very embarrassed expression on his face, and a short, cute, dark-haired girl grinning beside him.

"*A-hem*," Weezie coughed as he shuffled into the room.

"Go ahead, Weezie. Tell them," the girl said, her grin getting even broader.

Sam stared at her curiously. There was something familiar about her face. She looked a little like Dardanella and a lot like somebody else.

"This is . . . uh . . . this is my . . . uh . . . this is my cuzinthia," Weezie mumbled.

"Who?" Trudy demanded.

"My cousin Cynthia," Weezie repeated more clearly.

There was a moment of stunned silence. Then— "Your cousin Cynthia!" Dave exploded.

"Your cousin Cynthia!" echoed Sam. "Then who . . . what . . . who . . . ?"

"Who was Dardanella?" Dave finished.

"She's my best friend, Roxie!" Cynthia announced. "When Weezie read about the hoax contest, he wrote to me. He knew I'd be coming to visit, and he wanted me to pretend to be Dardanella. I liked the idea and I mentioned it to Roxie. She suggested we pull off a double hoax, if we could get our parents to go along with it, which we did. You see, Weezie and I haven't seen each other since we were little, so Roxie and I figured he wouldn't recognize either of us. And he didn't!" She looked at Weezie and burst into laughter.

"Hey, Weezie, it looks like this time the hoax on you!" Mickey called.

Then everyone began to laugh. And it was Sam and Dave who laughed the hardest of all.